By William
The cocker spaniel
With the help of his owner Bernice Glavin

William kept his diary for a full year to record his dreams and share his fantasy world with everybody around him. He hopes you will enjoy it.

Published by Elmvale Books, Wilton, Cork, Ireland
with the support of the Mercy University Hospital Foundation

All proceeds from the sale of this book will be donated to:
St. John's Men's Health Unit and Intensive Care Unit,
Mercy University Hospital, Cork

Mercy
UNIVERSITY HOSPITAL
**FOUNDATION**
Raising funds for patient care at
the Mercy University Hospital

ISBN 9 780955 484612

Published with the assistance of The Mercy University Hospital Foundation. This book is to be used as a fund raising venture for St. John's Men's Health Unit and the Intensive Care Unit at the hospital.

Design, Layout & Printed by

T 021 4354598 | www.barrydesign.ie

# Just call me William

Born in the country William the black cocker spaniel was adopted by a city human mother who couldn't stay still for long and had him constantly on the move. He explored and sniffed through wonderful doggie adventures as his owner secretly dreamed of becoming a rock star before 60! He graduated from eating sponges and chewing library books to making friends with both the lawnmower and the mouse in the garden shed. His helpful advice on dogfights, chewing, and doggy tails is not only valuable information but educational as well. He dreamt of roller skates and wished he could fly. There was the confusing day when the clocks were going back and he waited all day to see where they were going. There was the terrible event of a bowl of pot pourri mistaken for dog food. Excitement came with the arrival of a new human cousin and sadness arrived with the last day of the year. Thunder and lightening and trips to the grooming parlour caused near heart attacks. He even had a birthday party! Helped by his human mother and fuelled by his imagination William kept his diary for a full year to record his dreams and share his fantasy world with everybody around him. It is a diary interlaced with colourful insights into canine behaviour and interaction between dogs and humans. Dogs are deep thinkers as William shows. He hopes you will enjoy his story.

## Acknowlegements

For: My owner Ber who shows me love and kindness every single day. Thank you for keeping me company as we put my diary together. I appreciate the long nights you spent typing while I rested on the couch.

And for: My human sister Kate and all my relatives both human and canine.

Thank you to The Mercy University Hospital Foundation for helping me to make it possible to use this book as a fund raising project for St. John's Men's Health Unit and the Intensive Care Unit in the hospital.

A special "Thank You" to Alan Meek for such flattering photographs.
If only I could look that good every day!

Well done to the team at Barry Design for such an amazing job. The end result is absolutely superb.

"Hello" to all my dog friends everywhere especially Remus and Kerry.

The information and stories in this book are from my own experiences and life's adventures. For this reason my advice may not suit every situation so please be careful how you use it.

William XXX

# JANUARY

## 1st January

Hello, I'm William the cocker spaniel. I was born in Fermoy Co. Cork. I am totally black except for three white hairs on my left ear. My owner, Ber, decided I needed an important name so she called me William. Her Dad said, "nobody will ever call him William" but they did. Dogs are little people in fur coats but we can't write so that's why I asked Ber to help me write this diary and I gave it the title of "Just call me William"

## 4th January

If somebody asked me to name the five most important things in my life I would have to say my human family, my friends, food, walks and the weather. I say the weather as it can decide for me how far and where I can walk. No visits to the park on wet days, just keep to the road. Bad weather can make my life very boring and we get a lot of it. So I'll apologise in advance if I keep harping on about rain, but it simply can make or ruin my life. It rained all day today. Very strange as when I got out of my bed this morning and went outside to go to the loo the ground was cold and very slippy. I just stayed in bed for the day. Better be safe than sorry!

## 5th January

The rain has stopped. This is good and bad, good as I can sit out in the back garden and not get wet. It is bad as my bed was taken apart and everything washed. Of course it was all put back neatly and smelling very fresh. How can I explain that I like my bed in a mess and love to lie with my nose poking into lumpy blankets and rugs. Much more interesting as I can search for treasures that I know are not really there and find smells hidden underneath as I dream.

## 19th January

Got myself in a spot of trouble today. I found a book with a hard cover on the ground beside the couch in the kitchen. As I can't read (well not yet anyway) I decided to chew the book instead. So I started on the corner of the side with the picture of a lady on it. She looked nice and I discovered later that this was the back of the book and the lady was the person that wrote it. Ber nearly collapsed with fright when she saw what I was doing. Apparently it was a library book what ever that meant. I know she went there later and offered to pay for a new book. She told me the book was not hers and even if it was I should not have chewed it. I think she secretly thought that she should not have left it there to tempt me in the first place. But at least I had only just started and there were just a few teeth marks on it. Who said corners should be pointy anyway? Wouldn't they be much nicer if they were round?

## 25th January

We went for a two hour walk this evening. There were puddles everywhere as the rain had just stopped. Night time seems to last forever and I can't remember when last it was dry. Ber goes to work when it is dark and when she comes home it is dark again. She wears this big bright top when she cycles her bike and I think she looks like a bird.

## FEBRUARY

## 1st February

The ground was slippery again this morning. Then white bits fell out of the sky. Some fell on my face and melted quickly into water, before I got a proper look. Tasted quite nice though, but my teeth got a bit sore and my tongue was cold. Later I looked in my water bowl and the top was cold and hard. I think that was ice.

## 7th February

Ber is annoyed. The wheel of her bike keeps getting punctured. I think it's happened about seven times in the last three weeks. She says it's all the glass on the road and is very careful when we are out walking to watch out in case I cut my paws. I'm really very lucky to have somebody who loves me so much.

## 10th February

When I yawn I make a noise like a squeaky door. My nose stretches out and my face shakes with the effort. People always laugh when I do this. It really does not mean I'm tired as I'm lucky to be able to sleep whenever I want. It does not mean I'm bored or worried either. Humans get more oxygen to the brain when they yawn so maybe that is why they sometimes yawn when they are bored. I think I get plenty of oxygen when I run and walk.

## 15th February

Did I tell you I can smile? You might think that's funny but it's true. If you rub my chest I'll roll over on my back. Then just say a few nice things to me so my face relaxes and my mouth loosens. My tongue hangs out for extra effect and then I'm smiling. Normally I'm like a toy with a straight mouth. I know it's easier for humans to smile as they have more flexible faces. I need to be careful when I smile, as if I open my mouth and show my teeth it could look like a sign of aggression, especially if somebody who does not know me well is looking on. Most dogs have 100 facial expressions and most of them are made with their ears. Bulldogs and pit bulls have only 10 due to their breeding and this is the reason they can be misinterpreted by other dogs and get into a fight.

## 19th February

Heard a story about a dog in the films called Lassie. Lassie was sold to a rich person to pay for a family's financial troubles. It was in England and was 1938. She was taken to live in Scotland but escaped and travelled from Scotland to England to get home to her original owners having many adventures along the way. There were a few different dogs used to make the film but Lassie is still a hero in my mind. I think most of them were male dogs as they were larger and less timid. Then there was a Lassie on the radio with a human a few years ago. She barked by way of speaking the human language and humans made the noises of whining, panting and growling for her. Honestly.

## 24th February

There was a dog fight up the park while we were walking. Humans should not really get involved in dog fights but they still do! Usually one dog will back down. I suppose that's unfair but it may be a safer option. The two dogs fighting bared their teeth and jumped at each other. They rolled over and over, spit and froth coming from their mouths. Then they came to me and would you believe that saucy terrier from up the road bit my nose. What could I do but defend myself? Ber did exactly what she shouldn't and picked me up in her arms. My nose was bleeding. I had never seen my blood before. It was hot and sticky. A person ran up shouting but I know that's no good as the dogs will think you are joining in. You must distract them and then control them. Some experts say to pull the dogs apart by the back legs and tie them up separately where they can't continue the fight. Sounds a bit cruel to me. It all ended when a neighbour ran out and threw a coat over one of them. The poor dog must have thought that the lights went out. The dog "victim" looked everywhere for the enemy who was now inside the neighbour's house. He probably wondered if there was such a thing as magic after all as he was suddenly saved. Given the fact that he was smaller and weaker he would have lost the battle anyway. This way nobody won so they all still had an equal status. If a cross dog is looking at a human the human should turn to the side to show he is not a threat and would not fight. When you turn away he thinks you're saying that he's the boss and you don't want any trouble. You can stare at your own dog to control him but never at an unfamiliar dog as he will see this as a threat. If you yawn he'll think you are stressed out and may ignore you. But remember a fearful dog will still bite if he's worried, and the more teeth you see the bigger the threat he is to you. You have been warned.

# DOGS
by Maeve Mc Taggart

Some dogs are big,
Some dogs are small,
It doesn't really matter,
I like them all.

Some dogs are spotted,
Some dogs are dotted,
Most dogs don't dance,
But just normally prance.

All dogs are fun,
Love lying in the sun,
They really like buns,
Oh dogs are such fun!

(Maeve, my human cousin wrote this when she was nine years old.)

# MARCH

## 2nd March

I have big floppy ears as I'm a cocker spaniel. When I'm due a hair cut they are very heavy. If they get damp the ends can become very matted so they need to be cleaned with a soapy cloth and brushed so the ends are not knotted. I get the insides cleaned with a bit of warm damp wool. Floppy ears like mine are more prone to infection. As my ears are very sensitive great care must be taken if anyone is drying me with a hair dryer. If that breeze blew in my ears it would be like somebody running their nails down a blackboard but the sound would be amplified hundreds of times. Luckily enough that has never happened to me. My friend's Kerry has ears that stand up so she can put them back if she's afraid and forward if she's dominant. I've heard that in some countries people cut dogs ears if the dog's a fighting dog or a guard dog as he can't be caught by the ears and overpowered. How awful. I'm glad I don't live there. Other people pluck the hair from inside dog's ears to keep them clean. Yuck! If I had standing up ears I'd put them forward if I was looking for information and put them back if I was afraid. Wonder if dogs could have plastic surgery if they were not happy with their ears?

## 6th March

Why do dogs chase people?

Is it for fun? I mean humans expect us to run after mice, rabbits, and cats. So why shouldn't we run after them. I really don't think it's a nice thing to do as we might frighten some people. When we rush to humans and they make eye contact with us we take it as a challenge. Then we stop moving and they still look so we are still being challenged. If they put up their hands it makes them even taller and larger so it's even more of a threat. The humans should go down low, making themselves small and whimper. We would stop then, as there would be no eye contact and we would think we are the dominant one.

## 11th March

It's my birthday. I got a card this morning with my age on it. There was a badge for my collar. I decided to eat it instead of wearing it. That caused a big panic as there was pin on the back to keep it in place. I got a present of a squeaky toy and a new brush. My human cousins called and brought more treats. We had a human cake with two candles on it and they all sang happy birthday and blew out the candles. They told me to make a birthday wish so I wished for many more happy days like my birthday. Funny nobody thought of inviting any of my dog friends but we still had a lovely time. We all wore these silly hats and had these paper pipes that blew in and out and whistled. Didn't fancy them as they could hurt my ears. I had some of my cake and it didn't taste too bad. It was a good birthday. I know dogs age much faster than humans so at that rate in a few years they won't be able to fit all the candles unless they have a huge cake for my birthday. Come to think of it that would be a good idea as we could have lots of cake to eat. I think smaller dogs live longer than the bigger ones so as I'm in between I will be around for a lot more birthdays to come. They say the shape of a dogs face predicts how long he lives. Must look at myself in the next puddle I see and then get more information on that. All I know at the moment is that if you have a flat face you might not live as long as other dogs but as I definitely do not have a flat face like that bull dog up the road I need not worry. On the subject of him he looks like he ran into something and squashed his face but I better not go into that. On the same note bulldog puppies are sometimes delivered by caesarean section on account of their large heads but I had better not mention that either. I'll just be charitable on my birthday.

## 14th March

A lot of chocolate eggs arrived in our house with the weekly shopping today. They are for other people for Easter. Will I get one? I'll have to wait and see. Last time I saw an egg it was much smaller and it wasn't wrapped in shiny paper or in a box. Strange! I'm sure there was a different smell as well but maybe I'm getting a bit mixed up. I wonder if they will be cooked.

## 19th March

Today was a great day. A man came to paint the fence out the back. I tried my best to help as I know him and we meet when we are out walking. He has a few dogs and Ralph, one of his dogs, came with him and sat outside in the car with the window open, snoozing now and again. I was delighted with the extra company for the day. I made sure to be on my best behaviour for extra effect. I remember when I was young and the kitchen was decorated. The painter had an accident as he stood into the bucket of white paint as he got down from his ladder. He ran out the back garden in a panic covered in paint. I liked this man so I jumped up to welcome him out to my garden. As a result I was covered in paint too. The poor man got into an awful state and washed me under the tap in the garden and dried me with a towel. When it was all sorted everybody had a good laugh but it was very serious at the time

## 23rd March

Now I understand. Those eggs are special chocolate ones for Easter. They will not be cooked, just eaten as they are. I prefer the human chocolate to the dog type but I'm only allowed to have a small piece as human chocolate is supposed to be bad for dogs. I think the caffeine in it increases our heart rate. Supposedly a 20kg dog can eat 1kg chocolate before he really gets sick. Maybe humans just say that as they want it all for themselves. I know mushrooms and daffodil bulbs can make us very sick as well but there is not as much fuss about those. A visitor brought me some dog chocolate a few weeks ago and was very insulted when I didn't eat the whole lot right away. Would you eat something without a proper flavour when you knew there was something better around? Didn't think so.

# APRIL

# 6th April

I was standing by the fence in the sunlight, feeling happy and looking up at the sky. I thought I heard knocking. I looked up but there was nobody there. Yet there was definitely a knocking sound. I couldn't understand it. Was there somebody at the front door? But that was very far away. Then I realised it was myself. I was enjoying myself so much that my tail was wagging and wagging and it was banging on the fence behind me. Silly me. Don't tell anyone. Shush. It's our secret. Tails are just wonderful!!

My tail is short with black curls at the top. Sometimes it's thinner when I get my hair cut. I like to wag it when I'm happy and sometimes wag it for no reason at all. I walk around wagging and wagging as I have a good life. Dogs wag their tail when they are true and sincere but cats wag their tail when they are scheming and planning evil things. The way I wag my tail can tell you a lot about me.
I give a small swing to say "Hello"
I give a broad swing to say "I like you"
I give a wide swing to greet a special person.
My slow swing says "I'm not sure, I'm trying to understand"

Kerry, one of my dog friends, uses his tail to balance when he's walking along the top of the narrow wall between our two estates. He swings it over and back quickly from side to side like somebody on a tightrope in the circus. Puppies do not wag their tails for some days after they are born. If my tail turns in I'm not happy. If I keep it down I'm sad or depressed. If I had a big tail I'd keep it up straight if I wanted to be dominant.

If I was a dog detective I'd get my information under other dog's tails if you pardon my rudeness. Such an amount of information there. Molly the other black spaniel keeps her tail down when she sees me and sits down on it if we are stopped. She does not like to be sniffed so she keeps her business to herself. I will never understand women!

## 13th April

That crow is up on the roof again. If I bark he actually answers me back. The nerve of him and worse still he's standing on top of my house. If only I could get up to him. There's a ladder in the shed but I'm not too sure that I could get it out. The other day I caught him standing and looking at my bowl of food. Another day I was asleep in bed and he hopped right up beside me to get a good look at me. I opened up one eye and he got such a fright that I thought he wouldn't come back any more. But two days later he was back again as bold as ever. It's easy for him; he can fly around and get food everywhere. I wish he would leave my food alone.

## 18th April

Tissues are the most wonderful things. I love ripping them to pieces. I check sleeves and pockets to see if I can find some. I've now discovered that people keep them in their handbags as well. When we have visitors I sneak a look to see if I can find them. Sometimes they have different colours but I really don't mind what colour they are. I  prefer the bigger size as there's more to rip. Those rolls in the bathroom are much the same but there's a better challenge in tissues as you have to find them first. I even eat a small bit now and again. I have to do it quickly before I'm stopped especially if I am out walking and I find one as we go along.

## 19th April

Speaking of the bathroom....I went there today to have another look at this roll of tissue beside the toilet. Had a quick look in the shower as I was there. I discovered this little round, damp soft thing. Didn't know what it was so I decided to chew it. It didn't taste too bad so I swallowed it after a while. I now know it is called a sponge and is used when humans put that make up stuff on their faces. Why do they think they have to change their faces? If they were like us and just had a good wash it would save a lot of time, especially in the morning. An hour later Ber went upstairs and seemed to be searching for something. She looked at me but of course I looked back with my big brown eyes and she carried on searching.

## 22nd April

I had this funny feeling in my stomach all day and felt a bit unwell. Eventually I went to the loo and got a right fright. The small sponge I'd eaten had reappeared. Imagine in three days it had travelled right through and came out my "other end". Ber came home from work and when she saw the sponge went white in the face and got very agitated. She bought a new one and carefully put it away up high on the bathroom shelf. Every time I look at it I remember the fright I got out the back garden when I saw the old one after its journey to my tail. Ahem! I won't do that again in a hurry. Bet my insides are clean anyway.

## 23rd April

More rain but I got my walk. I think I'm having my hair cut soon. This is a good idea as my ears have got very heavy and tickle me when I'm lying down. My whiskers are so long that I can see them when I look sideways. My paws look huge but they are really quite small. I also get quite warm when the sun is shining. I can run faster when my hair is short as I feel much lighter and I'm not as tired afterwards. The only thing is that sometimes they cut my whiskers and I need them to warn me that there is something near my face. They also protect my eyes from objects. If you tap my whiskers I blink on the same side and turn my face away.

## 24th April

A visitor called today. I was happy enough lying on the floor listening to the chat. Then I heard them say that somebody was "barking up the wrong tree" Why would you be barking up a tree? Unless of course you were actually sitting in the branches. I enquired from Kerry, my dog friend and she told me it meant that somebody was looking at things the wrong way. O.K.!

## 25th April

There's a new kid on the block. She's a chocolate Labrador called Coco, absolutely gorgeous, sleek and shiny. Imagine she's got green eyes. I can't wait until she's grown up so we can meet up. The only thing is that she is much taller than me but I might win her around. We will have to wait and see what happens. Puppies are born blind, deaf and toothless, sleep

90% and eat 10% in the first week. They see at two to three weeks, and get their milk teeth at three to seven weeks so hopefully Coco is beyond that stage by now.

# 28th April

We went walking at nine p.m. I was glad to have a bit of fresh air as it was so wet yesterday that we didn't go out. I'm not too keen on walking at night as I'm not allowed run before we start off. This is because I'm so dark I will not be seen. I think Ber is just nervous that she will loose me. But I would never leave her as I love her too much. I got a present when I was small of a luminous yellow vest with silver puppies round the middle. Then I grew and it didn't fit anymore. We still have it at home. Another time I got a present of a red bandana but I only wore it for photographs. My lovely ears were never meant to be covered. Last Christmas my human sister, Kate, gave me an orange anorak with a grey fur collar. It's gorgeous but I really need very cold weather to wear it and then I feel like a stuffed sausage as I walk along. I sound like I'm never satisfied but I really love presents.

# 30th April

The grass was cut today. I had great fun as I searched for hidden treasures as I sniffed interesting smells. This is especially good if the grass is damp as the smells are released as the grass is cut. I am lucky as I can wriggle my nostrils independently to determine the direction the smell is coming from. I get lots of information that way. I roll on the smell to cover it with my own and disguise myself. I usually use my ears and the side of my face to do this. Just like perfume. Dead things have great smells. Sometimes there may be a bit of dog's dirt underneath the grass but I try to remember not to roll in that because I get myself into trouble not to mention the wash I might get later when my "new odour" starts to perfume the house. What's the problem? I happen to like it myself? Wonder if I could bottle it. I could call it Poo!

I remember once after I had found something interesting being sprayed with human perfume! Imagine that and it was a ladies smell and not a man's one! Anyway to get back to the lawnmower: I am always very careful when it comes my way. If my tail got cut off would they put it back? Be positive I tell myself and don't think like that. The lawnmower is kept in the shed where I sleep and it hangs up high on a special holder. I often look at it when I am having a rest. It is amazing that something that just hangs there for most of the time can do such work when it's needed and make such noise as well. It had a long tail that connects to a plug to make it work and it has this wonderful trick of winding back in when not in use. Wouldn't that be great for the dogs with long tails? The lawnmower and I are friends I suppose as we share the same home in a friendly silence.

I wonder I we could make something with all that grass. It seems such a waste to just throw it all away. I must think about it. Sometimes I eat a bit of grass to make myself sick and clear out my stomach. But I'm a bit careful about that as Kerry told me there are other green bits called weeds that taste very bad and make you very unwell. There are these other ones that are sharp and can hurt your mouth. We met a girl collecting them one day to make a soup called nettle soup. Why did she not go to the shop and buy some to save her the bother. Maybe she was short of money. Come to think of it I wonder if she would make soup out of the grass?

# MAY

## 2nd May
Today we went to the Lough close by and brought bread for the ducks. There was this huge shower of rain so we ran all the way home. Great fun! Even better when I was dried with the hairdryer when we got back. I was delighted as I was gently dried and got a few compliments as well.

## 3rd May
Ber is going away overnight. Her Dad will take care of me. I don't mind too much as I will be well taken care of not to mention spoilt. I even got a going away a present of a bone. I'm so lucky to have an owner that is so nice, and always thinks of everything.

## 4th May
Got on fine with my human Grandad! He fussed over me and waited for me to eat my food. The poor man. I am well able to eat on my own but suppose he was taking this minding very seriously. We had great fun playing ball and throwing squeaky toys. What a man. I like him. Ber came back in the evening and I was happy to see her even though I had a good time while she was away.

# 6th May

Today's the day! I was taken in the car to get my hair and nails done. There was even a nice blanket on the car seat for me to lie on and I was instantly suspicious. I knew something was up! I got such praise and compliments as we drove along that I decided Ber was nervous and a bit guilty as well. To tell the truth I was a bit worried myself but decided to act tough and not to show it. Once we arrived at the grooming parlour I hopped out and peed on the parlour door. Well I would look like a different dog on the way out so I decided to mark my spot as I went inside. I should not have worried as the lady groomers were very nice. They put me in a bath like the human one and shampooed me down. I was dried with a massive hairdryer on a stand. I didn't even mind when my hair was cut and shaped so I stood perfectly still. They even trimmed between my toes, and around my ears. I'm usually fussy about my ears as I feel they are my nicest parts but they made a great job of them and I was very pleased. I was there from eleven thirty to two o'clock and even made some new friends there. Some of the dogs there even got their nails trimmed but as I walk a lot mine were O.K. I felt really nice but was sorry that there was no mirror. I would have liked to look at myself on the way out and admire my new image.

Called to see my human cousins on the way home. They were delighted to see me and kept saying "Well, look at you" over and over again. Would you believe one of them said to me "William you smell like a man" Don't know if that is a good thing in the doggie world. I'm not too sure the humans would be happy if somebody told them they smelled like a dog. But as usual I said nothing, just gave my doggie smile and wagged my tail. When we got home I saw my reflection in the sliding porch door and didn't even realise it was myself at the start as my curls were gone and my hair was even shinier than usual. My little scraggly bits like a beard under my chin were even tidied up. I really thought we had a visitor, and hardly recognised myself. Of course to finish it all off my bed was straightened out and hoovered out. I told you before how much I hate my bed being tidied. But I know it has to be done now and again as there are these things that are called fleas that could live in dog's beds. I never get them as there is a special liquid that is squirted on the hair behind my head every so often. That awful smelly stuff called garlic is another thing that keeps them away if a dog will eat it, that is. After that all the windows in the house were washed inside and out. Has the whole world gone mad?

# 7th May

I stayed in bed most of the day. My new haircut is fine but I miss my curls. My fresh bed was actually not too bad. Those awful birds are still stealing my food. Maybe they think I'm a new dog and that they can share my food. I'll have to show them who's the boss around here.

# 10th May

I nearly had a heart attack tonight. There were loud noises in the sky that nearly split my eardrums especially now as I've no fur in my ears. There were crackles, whistles and a loud bang every so often. I put a paw over my eyes and peeped out from underneath. There seemed to be a bright light as well. Then I was told it was "Fireworks". I still can't understand if it was something to do with fire why that big loud fire engine didn't come. Lucky none of those planes that pass overhead were about. But maybe they just stayed higher up to be safer. It's hard to decide. I'm just grateful that I'm so low on the ground. I really am so nervous I cannot think.

# 11th May

There was mention of another outing. That car blanket was brought out and it seemed I was going to a dog show. I entered in the gun dog category and female handlers section. I nearly laughed as most of the dogs and their owners were well used to this and Ber and I had not got a clue. We only knew from the television that we would have to go round in a circle and go out to the judges when we were called. Fair play to us we gave it our best shot. We looked like two professionals instead of the two chancers we really were. We even thought we might win. Well aim high I always say. (I say this too when I'm trying to pee on a bush when we are on one of our walks) Sad to say we didn't win but another dog friend did. I got my photo taken holding the rosette and trophy so I could pretend I did. The picture is going to be put in a coloured frame at home that says "William" on the top and it's just beside the couch where I relax now and again. I had a long walk later so it was a very good day. There's always next year to make another attempt for that trophy, and I'll be more experienced next time.

# 16th May

Interesting morning today. There was a loud knock at the front door. I used to get excited when I heard the door bell when I was young and run like a whirlwind, barking and jumping to see who was there. Ber cured me of that by ringing the doorbell now and again when we were at home so I got used to the ringing noise and realised there was no need to panic. Today there was a man in a uniform standing outside with a box It was a present. The empty box was put down in the hall when the present was taken out. I was going to pee on it but I didn't. I was too busy trying to figure out where that man got the present he delivered.

## 18th May

I will never understand humans. Some new flowers arrived for the flowerbed in the front garden. I decided I could help to dig the holes for the plants. At last there was something I could do. But it was not as easy as it looked. I dug the hole all right but the earth was scattered everywhere and I got so excited that I stood on two of the other new plants and broke them. Ber thanked me very nicely but said she'd do it herself. The ingratitude of it. Why is she allowed to dig the holes and not me? My friend Kerry arrived and I felt a bit better and we chased in and out of the new flowers. I did feel a bit guilty when Kerry stepped on a few of the flowers but what's a dog to do? To finish off there were things called slug pellets that were to keep the slugs from eating the plants. Another way to protect the new plants is to put little containers of beer in the ground beside them. The dog that lived in the house before me used to drink the beer so that put an end to that that.

## 23rd May

Today we went online. Now for all my doggie friends: it's nothing to do with marching or standing straight. It's nothing to do with washing either. We are now on the internet so now there's no problem with staying up until four in the morning. I just snoozed on the couch beside two cushions and didn't even chew them. I was so, so tired. Imagine you can look up a site where you can put your dog's name and information if he dies. Notice how quickly I've picked up the lingo "site". No wonder I'm tired.

## 29th May

Today was a lovely sunny day. I must have eaten something nasty out walking as I got sick when we were visiting my human grandparents. Everyone made a big fuss of me, or maybe it was because I got sick in the house on the carpet. But anyway…I had a good sleep when I got home and was much better when I woke up.

# JUNE

## 1st June

Today I was lonely. I really couldn't say why. I know there was no sun and it was damp but I had lots of company. My outdoor mat was dry and

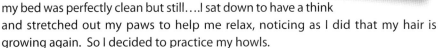

my bed was perfectly clean but still….I sat down to have a think and stretched out my paws to help me relax, noticing as I did that my hair is growing again. So I decided to practice my howls.

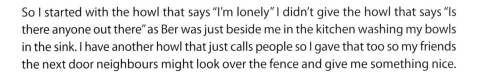

So I started with the howl that says "I'm lonely" I didn't give the howl that says "Is there anyone out there" as Ber was just beside me in the kitchen washing my bowls in the sink. I have another howl that just calls people so I gave that too so my friends the next door neighbours might look over the fence and give me something nice.

There's a dog up the road that has a howl that starts down low then goes higher and higher and eventually goes down low again. Sometimes all the dogs in the neighbourhood join in. We usually have a bit of a practice if the ice cream van comes by and the music it plays starts us off or else the bells in the local church start the chorus.

I finished off by giving my "I need help" howl even though I was fine but I just thought a bit of practice wouldn't go astray. It would keep those humans on their guard and I would find out how quickly they obey and jump to attention. Dream on! There is such a condition known as "separation anxiety" that some dogs suffer from. Apparently it can be cured by humans picking up their keys every so often, going out of the room and coming back again to prove that there is no need to make a fuss. It also shows that they do return. I wonder does it really work. If a radio was left on it would provide company and might help as well. If a person was really trying they could make a recording of their voice and play it over and over again.

## 4th June

Today a human friend came to visit and many dog stories were swapped. How we all laughed. I must tell you the one about the Christmas spiced beef. Ber's friend had a huge dog called Benjy. It was Christmas Eve and the family were going to go to bed early before Santa arrived. The spiced beef was cooking on the cooker. Mary and her husband decided to taste it and have a tasty sandwich for their supper. But when Mary went to the kitchen the meat was gone from the pot. She called her husband but he had not taken it either. They wondered and wondered and then looked at the dog. There was Benjy with the string from the meat stuck between his front teeth. He had taken the meat out of the saucepan without spilling a drop of water. He had actually put the lid back on the pot absolutely no mess, the whole spiced beef eaten and he'd have got away with it except for the telltale string. I don't think he got any Christmas dinner the next day as he had eaten it the day before.

Another friend who breeds and trains Rottweiler's says that a dog should be invited to eat. When I get my food I wait to be told its O.K. and then I give my Thank You" nod before I eat. I get the usual response of "You are welcome, enjoy it" And I always do. In the wild the leader always eats first and controls who eats next. In my life it's the human dog that is in charge even though sometimes he's not as strong as the dog.

## 5th June

Speaking of Benjy causes me to think back to when I was a few months old and had very little sense. Poor Benjy got sick and died at home with his human family caring for him. He was buried in his garden in his favourite spot. His two children owners knew he was gone to heaven, as he was a very kind dog. They waited night after night to see a star over the garden which would show that he had arrived there. Every night they checked over and over but it were dark and overcast so no star could be seen. Five nights later Ber and I were invited to their house as the children wanted to meet me. We all went out the back garden so I could be shown Benjy's garden and see where he was buried. Would you believe it there was a huge star shimmering way up in the sky. I was very lucky to be there when Benjy's star appeared to show he had arrived in heaven. I hope I won't go there for a long time yet. We went back into the house still very excited about the star. Nobody took any notice of me. A big mistake because as I mentioned earlier I was about three months old at the time! I found a bowl of very unusual food on the fireplace, very dry with a strange smell. So I started to eat. It was a bit hard to swallow. Then the shouting and the panic started. It was not food that had been left for me after all but a bowl of stuff called pot pourri that was used to freshen the place. How was I to know? I was young and didn't understand. It really didn't taste that bad. If I was a human it would be different as humans have much more taste buds in their tongues and it would have been stronger. When the excitement died down I wandered out to the kitchen and peed on the floor by way of an encore. Would you believe we still all are the best of friends and when a new dog called Poppy arrived in that house a small time after she came to my house to visit.

## 7th June

Today I dug a hole at the side of the fence. Some dogs dig because they are bored, want to bury a bone, hide something, cool off or simply escape. They may even do it because they are not getting enough exercise. I did it because I saw a spider going down a small hole and I wanted to dig him out. I made such a mess I never saw him again. Wonder if I killed him or if he is in that pile of earth I scattered. What if he's up my nose or between my toes? Just checked my paws and found a small stone but no spider. I heard once that if you want a dog to stop digging holes you should bury his poo down the hole he has dug. Disgusting!

## 9th June

Ber got a new bike. I'm very happy but secretly afraid for her. I know there's a dog that chases her on her way to work. What if he knocks her off? She sometimes puts out her leg to him. If he got a good fright he might stop. He comes very close when he chases her. Why does he not chase cats or even cars instead? As part of my training when I was young I was taught to be careful of bicycles, skateboards and cars. Some dogs chase postmen but I think this is a silly idea as you could be chasing away somebody who is bringing you something nice.

## 14th June

Thinking of bathrooms...

When I was young I simply could not work it out. Humans went to pee in the bath-room so every time I was in the house and wanted to pee I'd go up to the bathroom and go against the side of the toilet bowl. I was told I was right and wrong as it was a toilet but simply not for dogs. However a lot of people found this very funny and I was really very proud when they said I was so intelligent to work it all out. The problem was that a normal house cleaner was being used to mop up after me and the smell still lingered and it encouraged me to pee again. I eventually decided to do it the proper way and started to go outside instead. I just tip the back door with my paw to be left when I need to be left out. I still take a look round the bathroom now and again. It's a very interesting place.

## 21st June

Today is the longest day of the year. I believed that today as it poured rain all day long. I thought I'd never get out for my walk but eventually I got going when the rain eased off. It still meant having to stop and shelter three times when torrential showers lashed down. Did you ever hear the expression "raining cats and dogs"? Well today was that day. Imagine dogs and cats pouring from the sky. We would be walking on furry carpets. If we stood on a cat's tail he might scratch and hiss or if it was a dog he might growl or bark. If it got very wet the dogs and cats would fall and form a pile and what would we do with them all when the rain stopped? Hopefully they would just jump up and run away and not chase each other or fight. Just as well it never really happens so I don't have to worry too much.

## 25th June

I told you I am completely black. That makes it impossible to take a proper picture of me when I lie out flat. If my hair is long I'm like a hairy black roll. If my tongue is hanging out you can tell my top from my bottom otherwise it is quite difficult. Some bright person decided to put a pink ribbon round my neck for a photograph today to fix that problem. Imagine pink on me, a boy dog. If this gets out my reputation will be ruined.

## 29th June

Paddy, a neighbour, walks his dogs every day. They are walked at the same time so they have a routine. They are also very intelligent. Paddy forgot to take his key when he was out walking recently. When he got home he wondered what to do. Not to worry. His daughter's dog was inside and he stood up on his back paws and pulled down the door handle so the door opened. What a marvellous dog. I always knew we were the superior beings.

# JULY

## 5th July

There's a mouse in the shed. I don't really mind as he's up high on the shelf and my bed is in the corner. The only thing is that he disturbs me as I snooze as he likes to run up and down over and over again. I wonder if he is training for something. He's lucky as he can look at all those interesting bits and pieces that are kept up on the shelf so I cannot be investigating them. Tiger, the cat next door called a few times. It seems that she wants a look as well.

## 7th July

On a rare occasion I growl. I like to start with a small rumble in my throat as a warm up. Sometimes it means "Beware" or "Back off" like a threat.

If I get no response I pretend I'm getting cross. That dog up the road would attack at this stage but that's not my style. If a dog growls back I'm in trouble as I'm really very nice and not into fighting.

When I play with my friend Remus we growl at each other but we never show our teeth. We growl because it is fun and a good game. Some people think we are fighting when we do this but then they see us rolling and tumbling on top of each other and they know we are happy and are best friends. I also have a "request" growl that I use when I need something.

## 9th July

I saw a little boy playing with a stick today that made a loud noise. Remus told me it was a gun and humans can use it to hurt and shoot. I looked at the boy and decided humans stand upright so that their hands can be free to use weapons. What a pity.

## 12th July

I just love that leather couch in the kitchen. I lie there stretched out late at night after our walk and snore. Ber is usually writing or typing something at that stage so it suits us both. The arm rests are great. I put one ear on them and balance my nose on the side. What comfort. Every so often I get too hot so I lie on the tiles on the floor to cool off. Sometimes I even put my head under the curtains but that's not such a good idea if I'm damp.

## 19th July

Got a wash this evening. I stood in the shower on a human shower mat so my paws didn't slip. I have very definite ideas as to how my grooming should go. I like to start at my tail and finish at my head; probably the wrong way to does it but as I don't like getting my ears washed it keeps keep the bad bit until very last. I even tilt my head to keep the water and shampoo out of my eyes and a soft ball of cotton wool can be used to clean my ears. Then I'm dried with a small towel and wrapped in my own special one after that. I'm even carried down the stairs and that's a struggle as I'm not too light but I stay very still so I can help a bit. Once I put down outside I can shake. On a cold day I'm dried with a hairdryer but it was warm today so I was dry in no time. Us dogs are becoming more like humans every day. You can even buy dog toothbrushes and paste now. The toothpaste has lots of flavours like beef and chicken. It can be swallowed as a dog may not rinse and spit out if you ask him. Notice how I say "may not" as anything is possible. On a more practical note bones are great to clean teeth and are much more enjoyable as well.

## 22nd July

We spent the night looking at television. Or rather Ber did. I'm not too sure how I see it. It could drive me mad as every time I hear a dog bark I bark back. If I'm having a snooze I jump up quickly as I think we are under attack and I have to check and make sure we are safe. Not only that but I can't understand where the sounds come from. I tried to look around the back one day but saw nothing unusual there. I wish we would take it down off that shelf for a while so I could give it a good sniff and really check it out. I really don't know what I expected to see so I'm as wise as ever now. Where do the voices come from? Why are there no smells when food is mentioned and I don't think my nose is blocked as I can smell everything else so it's very strange. Dogs can see colour in shades of grey, green, brown or red as it helps us to find our food. Not that I really need to find food as mine is put out for me in one of my special bowls twice a day, Some people say that dogs should be fed once a day but as I enjoy my food so much I'm given two portions every day. I'm really very lucky. One final thing that voice on the television mentioned the Dali Lama. Is that a sheep or something to eat? Please get in touch if you know.

## 24th July

Today the sun came out. It was a bad summer so far. I sat in my shaded place and slept dreaming of chasing cars and eating juicy bones. As I'm a black dog I'm less tolerant of heat than lighter coloured dogs. But those dogs have their own problems as they can easily get sunburnt. But I forgot the sunny spots move around the garden. When I woke I was lying in the sun, my heart was beating fast, and I was panting. I don't sweat through my fur or from my skin. I sweat through the pads of my feet. If I'm inside I leave pawmarks on the floor when I'm warm. Any way I slowly got up and had some cool water. I'm lucky that I have three bowls of water in different parts of the garden so I always have a cool drink. When I finished I moved to another spot. I sat down with my head on my front paws giving a loud sigh deciding to have another rest. Would you believe I fell straight asleep and started to dream the same dream continuing on from exactly where I had woken before? If you hold your hand in front of a sleeping dog's nose he will get a scent and wake straight away.

## 28th July

There was mention of a soul, I'm getting confused again. I thought a soul was a fish or even part of a shoe. Is it something to do with a soldier or do soldiers have souls? Apparently humans have souls and so do we. Eskimos believe that dogs do not have a soul unless they have a name. Human names are just of one kind but dog name can be human and other kinds as well. Humans change their names when they get married or simply wish to. We rarely change our names unless we get a different owner. People who care about us give us names. It shows how important we are that we are named. Some animals are never named. How sad.

# The New Pup.

Boundless energy and endless fun,
He does not walk only run,
He eats anything from carpet to chair,
Will he eat the house in the end I despair?

He cries like a baby he loves me so,
Sniffing and scurrying to and fro,
His toilet habits I'm afraid to say,
Leave a lot to be desired in every way.

He follows his ball with breakneck speed,
Curly ears flapping typical of his breed,
He just loves toes to lick and chew,
An occasional ear will also do.

I just love him, what can I say?
I enjoy him more each passing day,
He thrills and torments simultaneously,
And I'd miss him if he left me.
Bernice 2006

(Ber, my owner wrote this for me when I was a very small pup)

## AUGUST

## 2nd August

Saw the strangest thing today. a kind of house on wheels but looked like a truck and there was a man driving at the front. At the back there was a holder with two bikes hanging on it. I'm sure there was a type of T.V. ariel on the top. My friend Kerry said it was a camper van and people go on their holidays in it. I suppose it's the same idea as the snail but he's a bit slower and doesn't use a bike. I wonder if I could get somebody to park one in our drive and myself and Kerry could sleep in it. Better still I could drive myself and Kerry around to interesting dog places and we could collect my friend Remus on the way.

## 3rd August

I would love to be able to fly. I watched a honey bee dancing and weaving today. I think they send out scouts to find the locations of the hives. I think the person in charge is the queen and if there are two of them one queen moves out to create a new hive. I wonder if all bees want to be queens some day? As the bee flew away a plane passed overhead on its way to the airport. The bees are lucky as they can take off and stop where they like but planes have to do exactly as they are told. When I came to my city home first I was afraid of the noise from the planes. I see a lot of them as the airport is not too far away. I like to think the passengers are looking down at me but I'm sure they are too high up to really see me. I always look up and wish them a safe landing as they pass. I know they are fine when about two minutes later I hear the sound of the plane landing on the runway. There is a dog relative of mine that is going to live in Australia soon with his human family. He is getting lots of injections and having blood tests at the moment. As he goes he will be on a few different flights and will be met by an arranged person at each place. He will be away from his family for a short time when he arrives but they will have prepared his new home for him. It sounds very hard but I suppose it's better than being left at home. I don't think I'll ever visit him as I would have to go through the same procedure.

## 4th August

Today is a bank holiday. I thought the banks got enough holidays but maybe I'm wrong. Humans seems to get an extra day off when one comes and I get an extra long walk so maybe there should be bank holidays every week.

## 7th August

There's another new dog in the estate. A real beauty, very unusual as he's a mixture of an Alsatian and a husky. He's only five weeks old so I'm not allowed to really meet him until he's had all his injections. I'll just have to wait. Such fuss. As if I had any diseases anyway. I probably won't meet him for a while as young pups should not be walked too much as it will cause arthritis and cartilage damage later in life. My new human cousin will be arriving in November. I can't wait. I hope my new cousin will be able to walk and run straight away but I'm not too sure as I haven't met many babies and anyone I've seen seem to be rolled along in little chairs with wheels. Maybe they get tired easily.

## Little Dog

Little dog snoozes, starts to snore,
Dreams he's at the library door,
Pauses a moment, what will he do?
He needs to join the library queue.

A little paw opens the front door wide,
Oh what a wonderful sight inside,
Thousands of books, every topic and kind,
Enough to blow his little dog mind.

Approaching the desk he waits his turn,
Excitement making his dog stomach churn.
A passing human thinks he needs specs.
Seeing the dog sign his name with an "X".

He tucks his paw beneath his chin,
So many books where will he begin?
He selects a book about a tabby cat,
And stretches out on the library mat.

Little dog wakes, becomes quite sad,
He realises the wonderful dream he's had,
But right beside him in his comfy bed,
Is the book about cats that he's just read.

Bernice
(Ber wrote this poem the
day I ate the corner of the
 library book)

Just call m

Wil

# Black Crow

A black crow sits on the garden wall,
His eyes are beady and very small,
Wings neatly folded are shiny and black,
He's looking at me so I look back.

His feathers are dusty, where has he been?
Can he tell a story of things he's seen?
If he could talk we'd have a chat,
I might even mention the neighbour's cat.

Changing position what does he do?
But lift his tail and "use the loo",
"Caw" he squawked as he flew away,
I said, "Call again another day".

Bernice
(That black crow called so many
times to steal my food that he
eventually got quite fat.)

# 8th August

Spent a very interesting evening. My human Grandparents called for a visit. My "Grandad" is very good at everything so he was going to put a CD shelf together for us. Of course everyone was talking and taking no notice of me! No problem! I am well able to amuse myself. I found this little bag with interesting lumpy bits and pieces so I chewed away quite happily. Apart from the plastic there really was no taste but I decided to carry on anyway. After a while I noticed everyone was running around and seemed to be searching for something. I looked up and thought they are a bit old for hide and seek but I suppose you are as old as you feel. Then I realised everybody was staring at me. I was still chewing of course but how was I to know that they were looking for the bag I had. It contained some things that would be needed to put the shelf together? Honestly these humans would wear you out sometime. Couldn't they have just told me what they were looking for or asked for my help? It would have saved a lot of time. Any way it was all sorted in no time and no harm was done.

# 16th August

Got a right fright during the night. I should have remembered the same thing happened before. There seemed to be lots of bright flashing lights and then there was this awful banging with very heavy rain after that. Ber said it was thunder and stayed up to keep me company until it was gone just in case I would be afraid. She is really good like that and that is one of the things I like about her most as she takes great care of me always.

# 17th August

What a great day. My human Aunt gave me some new rugs for my bed. One of them had long hair and will be great for digging with my nose. I'll be able to pile it up in lumps with my front paws and search for interesting smells as there are cats in the house it came from. I rolled and rolled in it once it was on my bed.

Such luxury and comfort. Of course you still can't beat the leather couch for comfort but as that wont fit in my bed the rug will do nicely.

## 24th August

Ber has gone to visit her friend so her Dad is minding me again for a few days. I know I will get really spoiled as she's is very fussy about me, and her Dad takes very good care of me. I give him a special look with my big brown eyes and it never fails. He falls under my spell and does exactly what I want. If I give him an extra look it may even work to get me an extra treat. Sometimes he knows I'm doing this but does not let on. It's a little game we play.

## 25th August

Ber is back again. I pretended to be a bit upset so she'd make a fuss of me. Very mean really, in fact I felt a bit guilty as I had been looked after very well.. We went for an extra long walk so I rolled in dog poo just to show I meant business. Then I started sitting down every so often. My own personal protest I suppose. I was sorry when I went home and had to have a wash to freshen me up.

## SEPTEMBER

## 2nd September

I pretend I can read minds. It's really a trick I have and very easy to do it once I practice now and again. Ber told me she'd a few things to do and then we would go for a walk. She looked at the ironing board as she spoke so I sat down beside it. She was intrigued. How do I do it? Dead giveaway. People talk to me about something but look at it as they speak so I know where to check. I just follow that look. If we are waiting for a visitor and they are late Ber may keep glancing at the door so there again I wait at the door. Easy peasy, simple when you know how. Humans think I am a genius. Well I am too. I can also sense trouble before it happens. This is good as I can give a warning. If a person is happy, sad, or frustrated I can sense that so it's not really all about mind reading. I know some dogs can sense that their owners are going to have a seizure an hour before it actually happens so then can help protect their owners by warning them before hand.

# 8th September

Ate another sponge in the bathroom today! I know I shouldn't have done that, but I did it anyway. Seems like I hadn't learnt my lesson yet. This time I was caught chewing. I had the sponge hidden in my palate when my mouth was checked so it wasn't seen. I even got an apology for suspecting me of doing something wrong. I was really guilty after that so decided I'd destroy the evidence. I took a deep breath and swallowed it down. I remember before I had a spot of trouble three days later to get it out the other end. This time I chewed it so its arrival might be easier as the previous time I swallowed it down whole but I will say nothing about that. Apparently if a dog eats something sharp they can be given cotton wool to swallow immediately after they do it and the offending item passes right through and does no damage as it will be wrapped in the wool. All I can say is that I will eat tissues but there would have to be something nice on the cotton wool before I would swallow it.

# 10th September

We went for a walk at ten p.m so it was too late for the park. The road and footpath run beside a large pond about two miles from our house. It is known as The Lough. Good smells can always be found in this area. Sometimes we bring bread for the ducks and swans. Why they just can't get their own I really don't know. I would actually eat some of the bread we give them but apparently "sharing is caring". Now to be quite honest I don't think of them until we pass by there the next time again so I'm not to sure I care all that much. Anyway to get back to my story. I found a dead bird so I picked him up and carried him along. I got some strange looks from the people passing us by as his head was hanging out one side and tail out the other side of my mouth. His wings were in front. I carried him very carefully as I was very proud as normally I chase birds but this was a rescue mission. My plan was to take him home and then to think out what I would do next. Ber had other ideas. She stopped in a gateway and tried to take him from me. She even offered me tissues to tear up in the hope that I would put him down. But I held on firmly but gently. Some people walking by were very impressed with my efforts. It was forty five minutes before we arrived home

and by that stage my mouth was a bit tired. I hadn't had my usual toilet stops and sniffing was out of the question as I couldn't sniff and hold the bird as well. In fact it was not turning out to be such a good idea at all but you know me, stubborn and will, never give in. Wonder what human I get that from!

I brought him right to the front door and into the house. I went out into the back garden pretending I knew what I would do next. Concentrate, focus and do not panic I told myself. (Isn't my English really improving? I have all these big words in my head that I like to use now and again) Unfortunately didn't concentrate enough when Ber offered me a treat. I put the bird down to eat and he was quickly grabbed and placed on top of the garden wall. Next minute a passing cat arrived and took him away. I pretended not to notice as I had no back up plan, and the notion of sharing my bed with this bird didn't seem such a good idea any more.

## 13th September

Knew I'd be sorry I ate that sponge. It re-appeared today with great difficulty but I will spare you the details in case you are having your dinner as you read. If you would like to meet me in person I will fill you in. All I will say is that it came out as it went in all in one piece. So much for my chewing experiment. It made no difference at all

## 15th September

Visited a house where the dog has a squeaky toy. He has this trick where he feels around the toy until he finds the squeaker and rips it out. He then makes a great fuss and gives it to the owner thinking he has killed the toy and in doing so saved the owner from harm. As he loves the toy so much his owner carefully puts it all back together only to play the same game again the following night. It has come to the stage that the dog is praised once he brings the squeaker to the owner. I think the dogs owner should be praised for his patience and understanding.

## 20th September

I think my mind was blank for a few weeks after I was born as I have no memories of those early weeks. So maybe that's why I can't remember my mother and father. I keep photographs of them both in my album. Those pictures were taken before I came to Cork. My Mum is a black cocker and my Dad golden so I take after my Mum. I look at them every so often and say that even though I look exactly like my mother I got my height and size from my father. I know I have two sisters and a brother all coloured black as well. I was the only one to become a city dog and Helen my first human mother said I got the best home. We text her on my birthday and on special occasions. She lives in Fermoy beside the river Blackwater with her family. There was a picture similar to the view from their front window on the evening paper once so I keep it in a frame beside my bed. It's important for me to remember where I came from. Puppies leave their mothers after forty nine days and I did just that. Helen sent her fleece with me when I came to my city home so I would remember her. It worked a treat and I never cried when I left home as I had my memories in that smell. As a puppy I used to drag it everywhere and it's still in my bed. I still have it even though I have eaten a few holes in it. It gets washed occasionally and the smell of my other home is long gone but I am very happy here and do not need it any more.

## 23rd September
Today my neighbour friends next door called and said that they'd found a big bird under a bush in the garden and buried him. It was the bird that I had carried all the way home a few nights ago. I could have dug the hole if they had only asked. It would have saved them using that big spade and getting earth on their shoes. It would be no bother to me. I suppose they didn't like to ask! Maybe thought I was too busy and had too much to do.

## 24th September
Today I was thinking about humans. Isn't it odd that they prefer sitting to jumping, yet they like us to stay and move at certain times. If dogs are kept as pets they have no job but to amuse and entertain. Of course others are kept as working or guard dogs. Yet we may be the stronger species as we pull sleighs, kill vermin, and even find lost people. In the past we were used as foot warmers in church and turned a wheel to help churn butter. Despite this some dogs are poorly fed and eat only left overs. We act as house alarms and we may sleep outside. (Now my bed is something else, but I've told you about that before.) A lot of dogs are not allowed on furniture or to sleep on human beds. Humans seem to do exactly what they want every day of the week. They can sit and eat when it suits them. They wear clothes. pierce body parts, get tattoos and spend money. We don't do any of those things yet we survive.  They think they should be in charge of us. I think we should be equal.  They probably think that if we were in charge we would sit and sleep as we like. Come to think of it that's what I do. Perhaps I am in charge.

## 27th September

Something was tickling my eye all day today. I scratched at it with my paw and it got worse. Over and over I got this feeling that something was touching my eye. Ber saw me itching with my paw and took a look. "You poor thing" she said. She told me that one of my eyelashes had got into the side of my eye. I didn't even know that I had lashes. What are they for? I thought lashes were something used in torture. Come to think of it I was being tortured all day. I know dogs don't have any eyebrows. But they would be useful to dust out of my eyes. I hope my eyesight never gets worse. I wouldn't like to wear glasses as they might slip on my nose and as my ears hang down I might not be able to keep them on very well. Dogs eyes are the same size all his life but his ears get bigger as he grows. The dog's pupil in his eye is very big with just a hint of an iris and as well as that our eyes glow with light.

## 30th September

Ber and I sat side by side on the couch tonight and she rubbed the side of my face over and over and told me what a great dog I was. Well I think I'm great too but it's nice to hear somebody else say it. Every time she stopped I'd nudge her to continue. Now and again she would move a bit but I would move after her, looking into her eyes to show how much I loved her.

Some dogs do this to show who's boss, that they are in charge and the humans should do what they say. But not me. I put my paw on Ber's knee to show my affection and appreciation for all she does for me. If I want attention I put my head under her arm. Cocker spaniels need a big amount of love and socialising and I'm lucky as I get a lot. Sometimes I lick her ear but I know she doesn't like that. In the wild the less dominant dog licks the face of the higher dog but I just do it to show love.

# OCTOBER

## 1st October

Do you know I can speak?

I think I could really speak but I choose not to. Dog language could be called "Doggish". Why would I go to the trouble of talking when doing something like tapping the back door gets the humans attention to help me do what I need to do? Humans understand us well enough and we can control them if we wish without using words so why bother? Even though we do not speak we still understand and respond appropriately unless we are misbehaving of course. We know the human language and all the words, back, stay, walk, come, sit, drop, no. out, ball, bath (yuck), and roll over. Dogs speak to each other with their bark but it's a type of secret code so the humans cannot join in. We say bow wow, arf arf, woof woof. If it is a low pitch be sure to stay away, but a high pitch come closer. So really we have the best of both worlds when it comes to talking.

## 4th October

Today I got a present when my human Aunt and cousins called to see me. It was a packet of sticks to clean my teeth. They tasted great and I would have liked to have eaten them all in one go. The three girls each gave me a dental stick as they wanted to have a turn to feed me. Felt a bit odd after a while. There was lots of rumbling in my stomach and I wondered what did it mean? Then all of a sudden I knew as I had to dash outside to go to the toilet a few times. I think I would prefer dirty teeth and fewer "toilets". Humans have strange ideas about your food. As I said before they feel you should be invited to eat. I always give a nod that says "Thank you" before I start to eat and Ber say "You are welcome. Enjoy". In the wild the leader of the pack eats first. And he eats his food in one sitting. Now that would catch me out as sometimes I like to have a break halfway through and have a walk around and a bit of a stretch before I finish off the rest. I have a few tricks that I do when there is food about. I am not allowed to beg from the table so instead I sit there trying my best to look sad with my big brown eyes. It always works and sometimes for extra effect I give a few sharp barks just to say "Hello, I'm here patiently waiting" My other trick is the one I do when my food is being prepared. I do a little dance by hopping up on my back legs and swinging around twice. I know the last dog in this house preferred nuts to meat. She might have been a vegetarian. I think most dogs like some meat. Do you know that our digestion starts in the stomach and not in the mouth? The human digestion actually starts in the mouth.

## 5th October

My friend Remus came with us on our walk today. We always have great fun running and tumbling over each other. Sometimes we run into each other as we get so excited so we both face each other front paws down and tails up high and play bow just to show it was just fun. We pretend to growl at each other but we are the best of friends. Usually when we arrive at the park I go through a gap in the fence and go over to the door of the house where he lives. If he's there he lets his human family know that I'm there by giving a special bark and they let him out. We run back to Ber who is waiting and watching inside the fence and we go off happily on our walk. Neither of us likes going home and when our walk in finished Remus is put back on his lead and taken back to his owners. But he has to be caught first and sometimes that's not too easy and he runs when he sees his lead as he would like to play forever. I think it's good to praise a dog when he sits to let you put his lead on his collar. People should reach down gently and easily to do it so the dog is not threatened.

## 9th October

I was very silly today. (Not again!) I chewed the edge of my rug. Normally I would not damage anything that I own except my toys of course. But a loose string in the corner of the rug kept tickling my nose so I decided to pull it out. Some of it stuck in my tooth and it took a bit of effort to get it out. When I was younger I thought my teeth were for ripping things up but as I got older I found out that was wrong. I know dogs chew if they are anxious or bored, because they like to, or are simply not getting the correct diet. If you are fed soft food you will want to chew. Puppies are like human babies as they like to chew when they are growing their teeth. Anyway the more I pulled the string the more it came out. There seemed to be no end. The piece around the string went into a little lump so I decided to bite that out. When I did that there was a hole in my blanket. A pity as that was the part where there was a smell of a bone I'd eaten sitting on the rug a few days ago. It's awkward to chew things sometimes as dogs do not have hands like people but I do my best. I heard of two puppies that chewed their way right through a kitchen wall to the dining room when their owners were at work and they were bored. There is also the story of a dog that chewed through the dashboard of the car as he was waiting too long for his owner to return.

## 13th October

We went out late tonight. This meant I had to stay on the lead all the time. This is because as I'm totally black except for the white hair on my ear. I could be lost very easily in the dark or worse still something could happen to me. The smells can be very good at night and I

pulled hard on my lead a few times forgetting there was somebody at the other end. I must remember I never walk alone. Somebody said if you can't see your dog's tail in front of you he's too far ahead. We don't go by that rule as long as long as I'm not pulling. That way the two of us are more relaxed. I know some dogs go ahead as they feel they are the boss but I do it to act like a bodyguard and to look out for problems and dangerous situations.

## 15th October

It was very cold today so there were lots of interesting smells. I was very obedient at the start and not wandering as we walked around the park. But then my imagination got the better of me. I ran and ran in the cold air my body was like a bellows as I galloped with one breath per stride. My ears were like wings flapping up and down. I realised what it was like to be a race horse. My back extended and my lungs expanded so I inhaled. Then my back flexed, my lungs were compressed and the air was squeezed out. Definitely I was a race horse in my last life. When dogs run their heart rate can go up to 274 beats per minute double the rate of the active human. When dogs snooze their heart rate can be about 80 beats per minute not unlike the human rate. Suddenly I came back to reality as right there in front of me was a deep pool of dirty rain water. Well as you know by now I never miss an opportunity so I started to paddle straight away. When I was called I pretended I had become suddenly deaf. The only giveaway was that my tail wagged and wagged each time I heard my name so it was obvious I could hear. But I carried on and then worse still I hopped over the fence in the park as I saw something moving in the bushes. Honestly I don't know what came over me. I walked on for a while but found nothing, vaguely aware of my name being called over and over in the distance. In truth Ber was back in the park nearly weak with anxiety, definitely convinced she would never see me again and blaming herself for not taking better care of me. At this stage I was aware that I was soaking wet and my paws were feeling cold. So I bounded back, my ears flapping and tail wagging at a fierce rate. I know Ber was relieved but wanted to kill me as well. But fair play to her she never gave out. In fact she gritted her teeth and praised me for coming back as she'd read in a book that if you punished a dog when he came back he would think it was because he returned and he might not come back the next time. Whoever writes those books deserves a pat on the back. Might have been a dog!

## 17th October

We took a different route this evening and I was a bit suspicious. Trouble in the camp I'd say. As we passed the vets surgery we stopped, opened the gate and went in. I didn't feel sick and I wasn't hurt so I wondered why we were there. My name was given to the lady at the desk and I noticed a few kittens in a basket but was too nervous to pay too much attention. There were a few other dogs there but we communicated silently sensing this was not a place to play or make too much noise. I was wondering if it was a happy or a sad place and really couldn't decide. Then a man arrived, very upset. His dog was out in the car after being attacked by another dog. He was covered in blood and we all stayed quiet as we knew this was serious and one of our own was in trouble. The vet came out and went to the man's car and we waited. After a while the man came back and paid at the counter. We were all sad as we knew his dog had died. I was getting more and more nervous. At last I was called and what a doing I got. I had my heart checked, my stomach felt, my teeth examined. Then I got my ears cleaned out before getting a few injections in the scruff of the neck to keep me healthy. Just when I thought I was finished (in every sense of the word) there was more to come. I was to be chipped! At that stage I started to shake as the only chips I knew were the ones we ate from the chipper. Surely chips were not made from dogs!! I started to perspire through the pads on my feet. But no I was not going to be somebody's dinner. Instead I got a large injection which was a microchip that had my details on it. Now if I ever got lost I could be scanned on a special scanner and a telephone call would be made to my home to say where I was. I also got a little medal for my collar to say I had been chipped. Not a bad idea.

## 17th October CONTINUED

It was all over very quickly and really didn't hurt as the scruff of the neck is where the mother picks up her pups to carry them with her teeth when they are pups so it's much the same thing. The vet instructed that I was only to have a short walk that

night. The cheek of him and me raring to go after all that. So I was just taken to the corner and home after that. I lay on the couch and really got spoilt after that so I pretended to be a bit tired so as to get extra attention. Apparently if I was in America I could get DNA taken from my mouth which could be stored in a central data base to confirm my identity, or else I could get a print of the ridges on my nose and store those. I like my nose the way it is warm and moist. Will have to ask Kerry about this
DNA stuff!!

## 18th October

There's more conspiracy about! I was taken in the car to a friend's house today. I really think that they were all looking at me but maybe they were just admiring me! Ber seemed upset and her friend said "He'll be fine. I'll give him the run of the house" She must be having somebody to stay. I have a sneaky suspicion they were definitely talking about me especially as they went on to talk about this visitor having a walk every day and having a choice of where he could sleep. I hope I'm not leaving home. Then again I've done nothing bad, well apart from that sponge, so why should that happen.

## 19th October

When I was young I used to pee in the house. But I very quickly learnt that this was not the correct thing to do. People said "Rub his nose in it, or even slap him". Ber didn't do any of those things. She knew that puppies thought the whole world was their personal toilet so she just kept patiently putting me out and I learnt very quickly with kindness. It is not good to discipline a dog unless you catch him doing the wrong thing. If you use a certain tone of voice he will look guilty even if he's not. If you are cross he will know you are upset and might not know why as our minds work in different ways. We don't ever feel guilt so it's no use telling us we "should have known better, asking how could you have done this to me"?

## 22nd October

Ber is a nurse. She minds sick people in hospital they don't have dogs there as it's a human hospital but a lot of what she knows can apply to us all the same. Dogs get sick and can have similar diseases to humans. We can get skin and ear problems. Our hearts and liver can give trouble. Our kidneys fail when we grow old. We get arthritis in our joints and our teeth fall out. We can be too hot or too cold, have seizures. We can develop psoriasis, cancer, have anorexia or suffer from excessive shedding. Our thyroid gland can be underactive a condition called hypothyroidism seen in 5% of dogs, first noted in 1970. We are unlucky that we can't get false teeth, hearing aids or have kidney transplants. However in recent times we can have joint replacements, chemotherapy and blood transfusions. A lot of our treatments are similar to the human ones even using the same drugs. Dogs can have acupuncture, see a chiropractor or have homeopathic treatments too. If a human pets us for a while his heart rate and blood pressure drops so we may be even better than drugs. We can detect that a human is about to get a seizure up to an hour before it actually occurs. It's a sign of the times that some of us even have our own private health insurance. It's good to see we are catching up. Wonder if they will microchip human in the future so if they got sick, lost or just couldn't speak it would be quite easy to find out who they were? Interesting.

## 25th October

There is talk among the humans that the clocks are going back. Why they need to go anywhere I really can't work out. I checked to see if there were boxes to pack them in before they went but there were none. As the day went by I walked round and round the house but all the clocks were still there. There was the big one high up in the kitchen that had hands like arrows with little pointers at the end that was quite loud. The golden one in the front room was there silently working as always. Yes that small clock in the bedroom was in its usual place. That one got me into trouble once or perhaps I got myself into trouble when I picked it up and carried it away in my mouth for a chew after I found it on the ground beside the bed. I finally solved the whole thing when that lady on the television late at night reminded people that the clocks were to be put back tonight, something to do with wintertime. So in fact they were not going anywhere at all. Problem solved. All I know from the television is that for the next few days it will be brighter in the morning but darker in the evening. I will say nothing and keep my thoughts to myself as I've already made fool enough of myself by thinking we were getting rid of the clocks.

## 29th October

I've heard of dogs that get so sad they do not eat. They loose their interest in the usual things. Dogs get upset just like humans and react in some of the same ways.

They understand when somebody they love goes away or dies. They have emotions, personalities and temperaments. They feel anger, apprehension, fear and also happiness, joy and sadness. They get distressed if they do not get out for days or if the weather is bad. But on a different note they cannot reason like humans so some problems are too big for them and humans have to try to understand their minds. Humans sometimes forget that dogs are social animals and their relationship can easily be ruined if they do not pay enough attention to each other. Humans take Dr. Bach's rescue remedy for stress and dogs can be given a couple of drops on their tongue or in a drop of water if needed.

## 30th October

If humans had dog habits:

Imagine if dogs taught humans a few tricks how exciting things would become. They would roll over, jump through hoops, and play dead. They would pee to mark their spot, and important places and their houses would be destroyed as a result. They would jump up to say "hello" and follow a ball. They would sniff out information and scratch the ground to spread their scent before they leave. They would chase things and be ordered to stay with the dog and then roll in interesting smells to bring the scent home. They know how to show dominance so I won't mention that. They could drag themselves on their backsides and eat awful things. They could jump up leaving muddy handprints on any one they met, especially the people with the most expensive clothes. The list is endless. We could order them to give the paw (in this case shake hands) do a High Five, or just go to bed when we wanted a bit of peace. We could turn our backs when they jumped up to teach them it was the wrong thing to do. The best thing of all is that dogs don't lie so if humans never lied the world would be a very different place. The list is endless.

# NOVEMBER

## 1st November

There was a dog barking in the distance all day long today. I wonder if he was upset or bored. Some dogs just bark all the time. I only do it when I need to. If I want to play I give a short bark, put my head down and my bum up high and I wriggle. I'm rarely bored but I give a small bark for attention now and again. Of course I give a bark to go out and to come back in. I don't need to bark for food as I get two good meals everyday. Finally I have my special occasions bark that I use in different situations. If I want my supper earlier I touch the bag of nuts beside the back door and give a gentle mannerly bark. It always works.

## 2nd November

A human friend got a young pup to keep an older dog company today. Can't decide if it was a good idea. We tried that once with a rescue dog but he had me backed into a corner in no time, and was very suspicious of people and children. He kept trying to escape even though we minded him very well. I would say he had been very badly treated. We had to return him to the person who gave him to us and he got another home where he was very happy. When a young dog comes to an older dog's home you must be very careful. The old dog will need lots of hugs and kisses. The puppy might easily become the dominant dog. You have to reinforce the older dog's position as the top dog. You can do this by feeding the older dog first and the puppy will know his place. Seems very cruel but the old dog will be reassured and not feel that he has to be aggressive to the pup. The pup on the other hand will know it is not necessary for him to be in charge and will relax.

## 5th November

Today there was great excitement as my human cousins got a new baby sister. I didn't see her yet as the only dogs allowed in the hospital are guide dogs. I could pretend to be one but as nobody asked me I decided to leave well enough alone. Some people are a bit wary of leaving a new baby and a dog alone. I suppose they are right as not all dogs can be trusted 100% but I think it would be all right with supervision. Of course not all dogs are very clean either so that would be another problem. I'm always kept very clean so when I'm invited to meet my "new cousin" I will be ready. Wonder if I need to get a present?

## 7th November

Spent most of the day licking and chewing on a large bone. My paws got a bit sticky but it was worth it even though they started to smell like the bone. I had to be careful not to chew them by mistake. A good raw bone is great to clean my teeth. I am never given cooked bones in case they splinter and damage my mouth or worse still my stomach. Some dogs do not like bones and might be given pigs ears instead but these are full of salt and can be fattening as well. I took a rest and an occasional drink of water to keep up my energy levels for the bone job. As I licked, I tried to remember how my mother licked me when I was young. I know it was done to clean and groom me. Sometimes I try to lick the faces of people I like to show respect but not all people like this. If I lick my friend Remus's face he will stand letting me do it and this shows acceptance. If he pushes me away I know he's in bad form. The same is true of dogs I meet when we are out walking so I have learnt to be careful about this.

## 8th November

I was on my second sleep this morning when something woke me. Couldn't really decide what the noise was at first. Then I heard voices out my back garden. Well it is my garden, but Ber owns the house. So the rumours were true. Tiger the cat next door had mentioned that the garden fence was rotten and there was talk of a wall being built in its place. Not being one for gossip myself I didn't pay much

attention and put it down to idle chit chat. But Tiger was right. The fence was taken down and two big trenches dug at either side of the garden. Well you'd have thought somebody would have asked me. It's not like that I would have demanded to be asked for planning permission or anything but I do have to mark my territory and boundaries and now these have been removed. As a result I was no longer "in charge". That upset me no end. To make it worse I was not allowed out the back all day. Had to pee, ahem et cetera out the front and it was most unsatisfactory. Then the rain came and the men worked on for a while. I got a quick look out and there seemed to be mud everywhere as the rain had filled up the holes. I know people in some countries take mud baths. Maybe the neighbours on either side might sit in them! It's supposed to be good for your skin but I decided against trying it myself as I'm black already so I'm not sure if the mud could make an improvement. Not to mention the trouble I'd be in afterwards or the wash I might get. Before they left the men made a temporary fence to keep me in the garden. Poor people! Do they not know I could dig myself out of anywhere if I really wanted to? But I decided to humour them and I pretended it was working for the next few days as they waited for the foundation to set.

## 9th November

The rain stopped and so I took a quick trip into the garden next door. I wanted to meet Tiger the cat to enquire about the next step in building this wall. As luck would have it she stayed in bed late and I got no information. Had an awful job getting back into my own garden through the gap. Didn't seem such a good idea after all. Won't try that again.

## 10th November

Ber went to work but she told me this evening that she worried about me all day as there was no fence to keep me safe. But where could I go. I mean the furthest I could get was into the back gardens of the houses on either side of us. But I didn't bother. I just stayed in bed relaxing and got out now and again to patrol the boundaries, or at least where I thought they should be. I could get a job on border duty somewhere. I'm sure I'd be very good at it.

## 11th November

I just hate the smell of nail polish. Why do humans feel they have to colour their nails? If they were meant to be coloured they would grow that way. They seem to spend a lot of time polishing and trimming their nails. We have a much better set up. When our nails are the perfect length they are like a letter "r" with the curve at the top of the pad. It they grow too long the nail can turn under and they look like the letter "p". I even knew my alphabet, well some of it anyway! If our nails are too long it causes pain but I think the human nails don't get sore, they just get in the way. Our nails bleed a lot as there are lots of blood vessels and nerves in the red part of the nail so great care has to be taken when they are being cut. As well as that it is difficult to stop bleeding once it starts and nail damage is very painful. Dogs with light colour nails are lucky as you can easily see the red part of the nail. Dogs with darker nails have a more difficult time as it is harder to see the quick of the nail and damage can be done much easier. The best thing is that dogs that get regular walks rarely need their nails cut as they are worn down unless of course they are always exercised on grass. I knew there was a reason why we never wore shoes!

## 12th November

Guess what happened today. Ber took me out to her friend's house again. She left me and I'm still here as I'm putting my thought together for my diary. I'm beginning to think that I might be staying here as she brought her fleece for me to lie on and a big bag with lots of my favourite food and treats. I realised while ago that my bowls and leads are in the bag a well. I forgot about it all for a while as Claire took me for a long walk and there were lots of new smells about. We are back in the house now. I'm after my dinner and it's getting dark. Ber told me to be good before she left so I'm doing my best. Surely I'm not sleeping here tonight.

## 13th November

Well I spent the night in Claire and Caroline's house. I slept in the kitchen on a woolly rug by the radiator and I sniffed the fleece to have my usual smells. I heard before that when I left Fermoy to live in Cork that my previous owner gave her fleece for my bed so I would not be lonely. Will I go back home again? I had the house to myself for a few hours as the girls were out, at work I suppose or school. I got another long walk when they came back and a fine dinner. Could get used to this but I'm sure there's a saying that says "There's no place like home"

## 14th November

Claire had a day off so we did some work in the garden. Still no sign of Ber. I know Claire sent her a photograph of me taken with her mobile phone. I took a trip and found a lovely soft bear and carried him down stairs. But I had to give him back as he was part of a collection.

## 15th November

More gardening in Claire's house today. I know Ber was afraid I'd dig this nice garden or eat the flowers but I do have some sense. I looked at everything but didn't do any damage, well except for an occasional pee here and there but that's only coloured water. You know I do a bit of digging at home when we are putting down flowers but decided this was not the place. I was sitting down quietly when I noticed a very nice dog ornament down in the corner of the garden. Funny place to leave it. They might have forgotten it out there. Decided to bring it in to the house but as I went back in I decided to have a quick chew on it before I put it down. A bit of a mistake really. I forgot to mention that Clare's dog had died a few weeks ago. Suddenly she jumped up and very kindly took the little dog from me. You see it was actually meant to be in that corner as it was on top of Benjy's grave. Honestly I should stop and think sometimes.

## 16th November

Still here in my new home. I'm wondering if I'm going to stay here for ever. Does the mouse in the shed miss me? Who will keep the lawnmower company? Will anyone tell my friends Remus and Kerry where I'm gone? Could they come for a visit? I'm trying not to be too sad.

## 18th November
There's talk of me going home in a few days! Hope I didn't dream that idea up! Will I know Ber when I see her? Will we get on as well as before?

## 19th November
Yes definitely something afoot but I'm afraid to get my hopes up too much.

## 20th November
Yippee!! Claire came from work and gathered my bits and pieces. We got into the car and Caroline her daughter gave me a big hug and waved goodbye. I held my doggie breath and crossed my front paws. But wait we were at another house. It was her parent's house. I wondered "Am I staying here now"? But it was only a visit. Our next stop was my estate. Home sweet home. If I started crying I'd be roaring and there would have been a track worn down under my eyes with doggie tears. But I just jumped up and down over and over and did my doggie twirls to show my excitement. Not to worry it was all O.K. I sat on the couch next to Claire but never took my eyes off Ber as I had to show some gratitude for the good care I'd been given over the last few days. But when we were finally alone I nearly burst with happiness and joy. Would you believe I slept upstairs afterwards- a new thing for me as before this I could do a little bit of damage if I got bored during the night? But I have given all that up. Got a right fright when I went out the back for my bedtime pee and saw the new wall had been finished in my absence. I pretended to be a bit put out but secretly I was delighted with all the new smells and I would have a lot of work to do marking my spots over the next few days.

## 24th November
Another book was borrowed from the library about dogs and it had dog horoscopes and birth signs in it. As I was born on 11th March I am a Pisces. I won't boast about myself but just say that the description it gave of me was spot on. It said I am perceptive, sensitive, adaptable, calm, peace loving, sweet, likes to please,

likes to be close, can sense when a person is upset, will sit beside a person to make them better, am an excellent swimmer and I love to jump in puddles. It also said I am very intelligent which I am. How else would I know that when a ball is thrown for me I must get it and put it back in front of the person so that they will see it and throw it again? Enough said I'm smiling with the compliments.

## 28th November

I leave my mark as much as possible when we are out and about. Tonight on our walk there some wonderful smells every where we went. The only problem was that a lot of them were up high and I had to pee up higher to be more dominant and leave my mark on top of the others. To be extra sure I scratched the ground a few times when I was finished as an extra signature. I look like I'm doing acrobats when I pee up high. I have to be perfectly balanced on my leg on the ground. I lift the other leg up so far that my whole back shifts over to one side. The leg up in the air is even higher than my head. The bits along by the edge of the footpath are like the news headlines but trees are the best. They are like gossip columns packed with news and information. The footpath is like a photograph of the past but the trees are the videos of smells. A smell not only tells me that a dog passed here, but tells me how long ago it was and what direction he was going. Earlier smells are weaker than recent ones. Water retains scent so damp days are good. Direct sunlight destroys the scent and high winds scatter it. I often think I would make a good police dog sniffing out drugs. I know dogs can sniff out cancer so I might be good at that too.

## 30th November

There was a man on the TV with a moustache. Most dogs do not like people with moustaches. I think it's because they seem to look cross. It's hard to work out what they are thinking. Maybe they have something to hide. They might be really nice people but you can't take the chance. So always be extra careful of people with moustaches.

# Man's Best Friend.

You cannot teach an old dog new tricks,
But I can remember when you were six,
We would waltz in the kitchen round and round,
Your nails made a clicking noise on the ground.

You ran and jumped and chased your ball,
You stood so proud all the other dogs looked small,
You hated cats and birds that stole
Your coveted dinners from your food bowl.

You sat in the sunshine as I lay out,
Occasionally walking roundabout,
You barked at airplanes passing overhead
And kept a squeaky elephant in your bed.

Nowadays your nose is a trifle grey,
The lovely gold colour is fading away,
Your teeth are sparse and some are brown,
And you give a sigh as you sit down.

Your gait is awkward your legs are bent
You miss the old haunts you used to frequent,
If you go out walking you come to a halt,
Your brown eyes say old age is not my fault.

You still hate lawnmowers, hoses and noise,
The garden is strewn with your now idle toys,
You lie down a lot and sleep in your bed,
But still love the touch of my hand on your head,

It tears my heart to see you mature,
And know for the old dog there is no cure,
But I treasure the moments we get to share,
And appreciate your efforts to show you care.
Bernice 2005

(Ber, my owner wrote this poem one sunny day as she sat in the garden with Beauty, the dog she had
before I arrived. They shared a few memories as they sat in the sunshine.)

# DECEMBER

## 1st December

The bus passed by as we were walking. It made a whoosh like it was full of air and when I looked it seemed to bounce along. It had a lot of wheels. I hope sometime I will get a spin on a bus as it's like a car with lots of people inside. Imagine one person can drive it on their own. I would like to go upstairs and investigate. Are there a few beds and a toilet or can you make a cup of tea and hang up your coat? I know some buses have music. How wonderful!

## 7th December

Last night I dreamt I had roller skates. Sara next door has them but it looks very hard to balance on them. In my dream I had two sets of skates as I needed one for each paw. The only thing was that I was not very good at skating and unlike humans I did not have a free hand to balance on the wall as I went along. So all in all it was a very dangerous situation. I pushed off at the edge of the footpath but each of my legs went in different directions and I kept falling down. At that rate I was going to break my leg or else my head as once I got going I could not stop and as my head was out front it was going to be the first part of me to crash into anything. I woke up in a panic with the pads of my paws perspiring with anxiety. I was glad it was only a dream but am upset all day today over it. I hope I won't get skates for Christmas. I heard you get what you asked for if you've been good. Well I think I've been good over the last year except for a few small mishaps like eating the sponges, or pretending to be deaf on occasions. Maybe a skate board would suit me better as I could keep two paws on the ground. Do they make them in my size? I will just have to wait and see. I might ask for a new bowl as when we were getting the new wall built the builder broke the one I got from America. I used that for getting my share of Ber's porridge in the morning.

## 10th December

I always said dogs were intelligent. I saw a dog walking along the footpath at the side of the road. The traffic was very busy and everybody was in a rush to get home as it was just getting dark and it was a cold evening. Suddenly the dog stopped at the traffic lights. What did he do but walk straight out as if the road was empty?

Would you believe it the traffic screeched to a halt on both sides? Both sets of drivers looked very relieved they did not knock him down. To make it worse he crossed the road without even looking right or left. He carried along on his journey tail wagging, nose up in the air tracking some distant smell. What a nerve. I know that in the Lassie film the dog would press the button and cross when the green man came on. I wonder if it was the noise of the lights that let him know when to cross. I'm not too sure that he could have seen the green man but of course it was Lassie and anything was possible. I won't say I'll try it as I'll probably get killed and anyway I'm never on my own crossing the road.

## 13th December

There was this piece in a book Ber was reading today about old dogs. (In case you think I was reading too she read it out to me) It said "Old dogs, like old shoes, are comfortable. They might be a bit out of shape and a little worn around the edges but they fit well" (Bonnie Wilcox). Hopefully when I am old I will be still very interested in everything. I know old dogs

can't walk or play as much but they still love their owner the same. They might be a bit more anxious as they can't go up the stairs, jump on the couch, or follow the owner about but inside their feelings are unchanged. When the previous dog in my house got old she had difficulty walking on tiles and wooden floors so there were mats and rugs everywhere so she would not slip and could walk as she pleased. Isn't that very thoughtful and kind. I'm living in a wonderful home. The longest living dog was twenty nine when he died in 1939 so I might live another twenty seven years at least. I will have some job blowing out twenty nine candles on my birthday cake if that happens. I'll also need a huge cake but I won't worry about that for the moment.

## 16th December

Ber brings her music along every time we go out walking. I don't mind really except sometimes it can get a bit confusing. Occasionally she whistles along to the tune she's listening to and I think she's calling me. As for crossing the road: that's another matter entirely and I hold my doggie breath. The reason is that Ber can sometimes forget where we are and I'm sure on occasions might even start dancing if we had enough time. The secret is that I'm sure she fancies herself as a rock star. But tonight beat all. We were ambling along the way we do. Me having numerous sniffs and intermittent pees and Ber on the stage with her band (in her dreams) Next minute I heard "Just look over your shoulder" so I did and saw nothing unusual. Again "Just look over your shoulder", still nothing unusual. "Just look over your shoulder and I'll be there. " I'm getting sick of this as I was on the lead with Ber behind so where else would she be? Then I realised she was singing and not talking to me. I gave a final check and nearly died of mortification. There was a man walking along behind us listening to the singing. Ber nearly choked when she saw him. I decided to pretend to be just a dog for once instead of being half human. But ten minutes passed and "Just look over your shoulder, just look over your shoulder" Honestly I'm going to bed tonight with a stiff neck from all this turning around. I'll give that Phil Collins a run for his money if I ever meet him for writing that song. He'll be travelling so fast that looking over his shoulder will be the last thing on his mind as he will be too busy looking ahead watching where he's going as I charge along behind him.

## 19th December

Something great is going to happen I think but I'm not sure what it is yet. People have put bright lights on their houses. There are big inflatable Santas in the front gardens and lots of decorations on windows. One house has even a flashing Santa on its chimney. Imagine this evening as we passed the lake where we feed the swans there is a crib with music playing. How do the birds sleep with the light and the music? Maybe they just dance the night away. There are little signs in gardens that say "Santa please stop here" as I mentioned before I hope he will come to me. I think I've been good.. But I'm still thinking: what about the time I ate the sponge, or ripped up the tissues, or tore up my blanket in my bed or chewed the sock that had fallen from the laundry basket. I think I may be in trouble. I'll just have to hope for the best. I will just put it out of my mind as I'm beginning to get boring going over my "sins" again and again.

## 23rd December

Christmas is coming and the man on the radio said today that Santa is on his way. I know he comes at night so I haven't met him so far. Last year I tried to stay awake but closed my eyes for ten seconds in the middle of the night. Would you believe it I missed him and when I woke my presents were there. I got a new blanket for my bed, a ball, a stuffed toy, and a Christmas stocking. I also got a lovely dinner on Christmas day so I can't wait for this Christmas. I will stay awake this time though.

## 24th December

I must go to bed early tonight as I don't want to be still up when Santa arrives. I mean what would I do. I'm supposed to be on guard so if I was to do the right thing I should bark and chase him away. Somehow I don't think this is the right thing to do in this case. Imagine if I met Rudolf, "what would I say?". Well I couldn't mention his nose as it would be very rude but I suppose I could check that it glowed. I think no matter what happens I will stay in bed all night and then I won't upset anyone. But I still plan on staying awake all night. I got Ber to hang up my stocking by the fireplace. I hoped silently to myself that my letter made it safely to the North Pole. I'm not too sure it was a good idea to give it to my friend Kerry to post as he has a habit of eating paper. It is now eight o' clock and I'm absolutely exhausted as I have worried all day about Santa. A final thing if he wants to land in the drive instead of on the roof the car is parked in his way.  Hopefully he will figure something out!

## 25th December

I had a lot of dreams last night. It was still dark when I heard my name being called. I discovered I had been dreaming and was crying in my sleep I went for another quick snooze and then went down to check out if Santa had arrived. Would you believe it there was a parcel with my name on it and a new blanket for my bed inside. The stocking that I had left was full of dog biscuits and chewy treats. Just beside my bowl was a new ball and a box of dog biscuits. Imagine they were my favourite kind Marrowbone Roll Treats like they sell in Tesco's. Santa is truly magic. I got even more presents later from my human relatives: a big rubber squeaky pig toy and a Christmas stocking with lots of nice goodies inside. The best of it all was that I had a lovely dinner as Christmas Day is a day for nice dinners

## 26th December

I was very tired all day today after all the Christmas excitement, but also because it was Ber's birthday. I would have liked to have given her a metal badge with her age on it but the shops were closed for the day. I didn't have much money left after Christmas so that was another problem. Couldn't ask for a loan without explaining the reason why... Some wonderful presents arrived in the house but the best was a huge bunch of flowers with such beautiful colours. I sat beside them out in the hall and closed my eyes and dreamt of summer as I caught their wonderful smell. For extra effect I leant on the radiator to pretend I was sitting in the sun. If someone sang that song now that asked "Where are all the flowers gone?" I would have to answer that they are all in our house as there seems to be so many of them here. How wonderful! All we're short now are a few butterflies!

## 28th December

Santa must be at home in bed by now. What a pity he never stays too long but as he has so much to do he must keep going. I'm sure he just takes a few days rest and starts all over again in order to be ready for the next Christmas. I can't help but admire the man. He must get very warm when he goes to the hot countries. I know I feel that way when my hair has grown long in the warm days. Maybe I could go and visit Santa some time during the year. What if we used sleighs instead of buses and cars so there would be very little traffic on the roads. The only thing is that there would be no traffic lights in the sky so it might be a bit hard to keep some control. I'm not sure our weather is good enough for sleighs all the year round and those parking spaces up in Tesco's would have to be made bigger.

## 30th December

I'm getting a bit panicky today for two reasons. The first is because I got this awful daft idea. You know that song about the twelve days of Christmas and the "true love" gave lots of presents? Well I had a thought if all the presents arrived together and Ber was not at home I would have to entertain, not to mention tidy up after drummers drumming, pipers piping, leaping lords and dancing ladies. That would be bad enough but imagine sharing my bed with laying geese, calling birds, turtle doves, French hens and finding a partridge in a pear tree (which we haven't got) outside the door. I could share the gold rings with my dog friends. Enough of that. I'm really trying to distract my thoughts from the fact that tomorrow is the last day of the year and my year of writing this diary will have come to an end. How the year has flown past.

## 31st December

Well it's officially here. The last day has arrived. There seems to be an air of excitement about. I think humans are strange. They think because a new year is coming that everything will automatically change for the better. I'm sure when they realise that everything is the same after a few days that it is very upsetting. I know most of these New Year resolutions only last a short time. But I have one of my own believe it or not. I plan to use my diary to make money for a good cause. It might be ambitious but I'm going to try. So tonight when I'm shivering and shaking every time a firework goes off I will try to stay calm and think positive thoughts. We are moving on into the New Year to make new beginnings, keep up good friendships and try to be even nicer to people. So all is not lost. I hope you enjoyed reading my stories. I know I loved telling them. Woof, Woof to you all.

Love you.

WILLIAM XXXX